THE GOLDEN ARMOUR

ClaW
THE GIANT
MONKEY

D1442730

With special thanks to Lucy Courtenay

For my very own Beasts, Alfie and George

www.beastquest.co.uk

ORCHARD BOOKS
338 Euston Road, London NW1 3BH
Orchard Books Australia
Level 17/207 Kent St, Sydney, NSW 2000

A Paperback Original
First published in Great Britain in 2008

Beast Quest is a registered trademark of Working Partners Limited
Series created by Working Partners Limited, London

Text © Working Partners Limited 2008
Cover illustration © David Wyatt 2008
Inside illustrations © Orchard Books 2008

A CIP catalogue record for this book is available
from the British Library.

ISBN 978 1 84616 989 2

9 10 8

Printed and bound in China by Imago

The paper and board used in this paperback are natural recyclable
products made from wood grown in sustainable forests. The
manufacturing processes conform to the environmental regulations
of the country of origin.

Orchard Books is a division of Hachette Children's Books,
an Hachette UK company.

www.hachette.co.uk

ClaW
THE GIANT
MONKEY

BY ADAM BLADE

ORCHARD BOOKS

Did you think it was over?

Did you think I would accept defeat, and disappear?

No! That can never be. I am Malvel, the Dark Wizard who strikes fear into the hearts of the people of Avantia. I still have much more to show this kingdom, and one boy in particular – Tom.

The young hero liberated the six Beasts of Avantia from my curse. But his fight is far from over. Let us see how he fares with a new Quest, one that will surely crush him and his companion, Elenna.

Avantia's Beasts had good hearts that I corrupted for my own wicked purpose. Now, thanks to Tom, they are free to protect the kingdom once more. But I have created six new supreme Beasts whose hearts are evil and so cannot be set free: monster squid, giant monkey, stone charmer, snake man, king of spiders and three-headed lion. Each one guards a piece of the most precious relic of Avantia, which I have stolen: the suit of golden armour that gives magical strengths to its rightful owner. I will stop at nothing to prevent Tom collecting the complete suit and defeating me again. This time he will not win!

Malvel

PROLOGUE

The air was hot and humid. The market trader mopped his brow and stared into the thick mass of jungle trees before him. It reminded him of rotten black teeth. Heavy vines hung down like snakes.

"Do we have to go there?" asked the boy at the trader's side. "Is there no other way?"

"We've travelled hundreds of miles

for the Ruby Guya fruit," the trader reminded his assistant. "It grows nowhere else in Avantia. Only here in the Dark Jungle."

"But aren't there monsters who live here? That's what people say," the boy whispered.

Everyone in Avantia knew the terrors of the Dark Jungle: creatures that plucked men from the ground and ate them whole; plants whose rich scents could overwhelm a person at twenty paces. Few dared to enter – and fewer still returned.

"Rumours to frighten honest men," said the trader with a wave of his hand.

"Is it true the Ruby Guya possesses miraculous powers?" the boy asked.

The trader nodded. "One bite of its sweet red flesh brings courage to the faint-hearted and strength to the weak," he said. "It is only ever seen at the king's table, and fetches a price beyond gold." He glanced at his young assistant. "But we must keep our heads if we are to harvest it. Do you understand?"

The boy swallowed his fear and nodded.

They entered the jungle side by side. At once the light grew dim. The ground was marshy beneath their feet and there was a stench of rotting vegetation. Birds screamed and wheeled overhead. Great tree ferns arched above them, their leaves a bright and poisonous green.

The trader gazed at the fleshy jungle flowers that hung in ropes from the trees. They smelled over-ripe and dangerous. He forced all thoughts of creatures and deadly scents from his mind. But he couldn't shake the feeling that something was watching them.

A branch crashed to the ground. The trader whirled, pulling his knife from its sheath in one swift movement. But all he saw were shadows.

They walked on. Soon they found themselves wading through a foul-smelling swamp. The thick, pungent water lapped at their knees. The trader clenched his teeth to stop himself from trembling. Who knew what vile creatures lurked at his feet?

He wanted to weep with relief when they touched solid ground again.

"We must press on," he said.

The boy crawled out of the swamp. "Leeches," he sobbed. "They're all over my legs!"

The trader prised the leeches from the boy's bare ankles with the blade of his knife. Shuddering, he did the same to the bloodsuckers on his own limbs. The Dark Jungle was a terrible, stinking place. He would be glad to leave – once he had found the fruit he sought.

They moved on. Shafts of sunlight seemed to drip to the ground like venom. Monkeys chattered in the highest treetops above them. It sounded as if they were laughing.

At last, through the ferns, the trader glimpsed a cluster of trees with green, waxy leaves and plump red fruits. His heart leapt.

The Ruby Guya!

The trader hauled himself into the nearest tree, laughing with delight.

"Come on, boy!" he called behind him. "This fruit is ripe for the picking. Where are you?"

He looked back over his shoulder. The boy had disappeared. Uneasy now, the trader glanced around the clearing. Something was not right.

There was a scuffling sound in the undergrowth – and then a scream. The trader froze.

Suddenly a fist of gnarled claws shot out of the foliage and grabbed the fruit from the trader's hand. The man screamed as a hairy face with bloodshot eyes emerged from behind the green leaves. Huge lips curled back to reveal thick, yellow teeth.

"Boy!" the trader croaked. "Run!"

Then his eyes darted to the jungle floor and what he saw made his blood run cold. All that remained of his companion were strips of torn linen from the boy's tunic.

Slowly, the trader looked back at the Beast. It was too late for escape. He howled as a long, thick tail with a deadly claw on its tip flicked out and wrapped itself round his waist.

The trader's screams echoed around the jungle clearing. Then he was gone.

CHAPTER ONE

CROSSING THE WINDING RIVER

Tom guided his black stallion Storm inland, away from Avantia's western shore. Elenna sat quietly behind him, her arms around his waist. Silver, Elenna's pet wolf, padded quietly alongside. Struggling with Zepha the monster squid had been their toughest challenge yet. If it hadn't been for Sepron, the great sea serpent and protector of Avantia's waters, they might never have defeated the evil Beast.

Stored safely in Storm's saddlebag lay a magnificent golden helmet, shaped like the head of an eagle. It was the first piece from the great suit of golden armour, which gave magical powers to its rightful owner. The armour had belonged to the Master of the Beasts and had been destined to pass to Tom as a reward for completing his first Quest. Now it was Tom's fate to recover the six pieces, which had been stolen by the Dark Wizard Malvel and scattered across Avantia. But Malvel had created six evil Beasts to protect each piece. Zepha had been the first, with the helmet as the prize. There were five more Beasts to overcome and five pieces of armour to collect.

But that was not all. For Malvel had taken more than the armour. He had kidnapped Aduro, King Hugo's wizard and Tom and Elenna's friend and protector.

"I'm worried about Aduro," Elenna said now.

"That's why we have to find and defeat this next Beast, Claw, whatever he is," said Tom. "We will soon find all six pieces of the armour and, when our Quest is complete, we will rescue Aduro. As he told us himself, there's no other way!"

Silver yapped in excitement, and Storm tossed his fine head.

"Malvel may have Aduro," said Tom," but we still have Aduro's enchanted map. Let's see if it will tell us where we can find Claw."

They dismounted and Tom drew the parchment scroll from the saddlebag.

As he unrolled it, the map sprang to life. The mountains of Avantia rose as high as his thumb and tiny waves crashed on the map's shores. Tom and Elenna shared a smile. No matter how many times they used the magical map, it never failed to amaze them.

Slowly the image on the map began to slide down, revealing new terrain in the south. The landscape grew greener. Suddenly a glowing red line appeared from Avantia's western shore and snaked down, past the Winding River, into a small patch of green in the south east.

Elenna put her finger to the spot, then started and pulled her hand away in surprise. Her finger was warm and damp.

"I have an idea where we might be headed," said Tom, frowning.

"There's a place called the Dark Jungle

in the south east. The people of Avantia rarely go there."

"Why not?" Elenna asked.

"The Dark Jungle is dangerous as well as hot," Tom told her. "Strange creatures live in it. There are poisonous plants and spiders the size of your head. I've heard that if the heat and the insects don't kill you, the creatures will."

Elenna shuddered.

Tom studied the map more closely. Something was moving in the depths of the Dark Jungle. It glimmered, then disappeared again.

"Look," Tom said, showing Elenna the map. "Can you see? That tiny gold dot. Look closely."

"It's the chainmail!" Elenna said in excitement. "The next piece of the armour!"

Tom rolled up the map. "We're

going to the Dark Jungle," he said.
"There's no time to lose!"

Tom, Elenna, Storm and Silver
headed further inland, towards the
Winding River. With the sun on their
backs and wonderful views of Avantia
all around them, it was easy to forget
the danger of their Quest.

They followed the road down
into a green valley. Tom took out the
map again and studied their position,
tracing the red line towards the
Dark Jungle.

When he had looked the first time,
the tiny golden chainmail had been
near the mouth of the jungle. Now it
was deep among the trees.

Had Malvel moved it?

Tom's heart thumped.

Did he know they were coming?

They carried on. The road led deep
into the valley. Soon Tom and Elenna
could see the gleaming ribbon of
water that was the Winding River. The
riverbank twisted and turned like
a writhing snake, and the water was
turning gold in the late-afternoon sun.

But the road stopped abruptly at the river's edge and there was no sign of a bridge. The water rushed past them, wild and foaming. It looked dangerous.

Carefully, Tom took the golden helmet from the saddlebag. It shone in the sunlight as if it were made of fire. His heart beating fast, Tom raised it above his head and slowly pulled it down over his face.

At once, his eyesight sharpened. He could see every blade of grass along the riverbank and, when he looked downstream, he saw the river stretching away for miles. Everything was crystal clear.

"Can you see anything?" Elenna asked.

"I can see *everything*," Tom said in wonder. "It's amazing! But I can't see a bridge."

"The river twists away behind those trees," said Elenna, pointing upstream. "Perhaps there is a bridge somewhere out of sight."

As they followed the river, Tom began to feel worried. The light was fading rapidly now and he felt they had to cross the water before nightfall.

They rounded another twist in the river. Silver barked.

"There!" Elenna shouted.

At last, a bridge.

But it looked old. The planks were warped, rickety and broken in several places, and some were missing entirely, like teeth in an old witch's mouth. The water swirled below, white and furious.

"It won't take our weight if we cross together," said Tom, jumping from Storm. "But if we go one at a time, we might make it. Elenna, get Silver over first."

In three bounds, Silver was across. The bridge creaked and swayed, but stayed in one piece.

Tom gave Elenna an encouraging nod as she stepped on to the bridge. One of the planks cracked and fell into the water as she leapt for the shore. But she made it.

"Come on, Storm," Tom coaxed, trying to sound confident. "You next."

But the stallion was spooked by the swirling water and refused to move.

Tom stepped on to the bridge, testing the plank with his weight. The twisted wood creaked under his feet, but didn't break.

"Come on, boy," Tom called softly, holding out his hand.

The stallion stepped forward. The wooden slats groaned in protest and the bridge swayed. Storm rolled his eyes in terror, as Tom struggled to keep him calm and urge the horse forward.

A rotten plank snapped just as Storm's last back hoof lifted from it. Then the entire section of the bridge they had been standing on crumbled into the angry, churning water below.

"We need to lighten the load," Tom called over his shoulder to Elenna.

Very slowly, he sank to his knees to
spread his weight. Then he unfastened
his helmet, shield and sword.

"Catch!"

The bridge groaned again as Tom
threw everything towards Elenna.
Now he had no magic to protect him.
Only his wits.

Tom edged forward but the planks
splintered. He could only watch in
horror as the groaning bridge began
to fall away.

"Come on, Storm!" he shouted, scrambling towards the shore.

But the stallion threw back his head and whinnied in terror as the bridge collapsed beneath him.

"No!" Elenna screamed from the riverbank.

But it was too late. Tom and Storm had fallen into the deadly water!

CHAPTER TWO

ORDEAL IN THE WATER

Tom felt himself being dragged under the surface. The water was cold and the current strong. He could sense Storm panicking and thrashing his legs. With a lunge, Tom grabbed hold of the stallion's reins.

Half-blinded and choking, he somehow broke the surface of the river. "Throw me my sword!" he shouted to Elenna.

The heavy sword flew through the
air and plunged into the water beside
him. Storm kicked wildly. With
a mighty effort, Tom reached out and
grabbed hold of the hilt before the
sword sank out of sight. His lungs
were burning as he stabbed his
sword into the riverbank with all
his might and held on. The power of

the current and Storm's weight almost dragged Tom away. But he kept his grip on the sword, and the blade held fast in the ground.

"Tom!" Elenna called, running to the edge of the river and holding out her hand.

He kicked hard, and felt solid ground just in front of him. His feet slithered through the mud, and the water sucked at his legs. Grunting with the effort, Tom grabbed Elenna's outstretched hand. Then he swung himself on to the bank and collapsed on the grass, Storm's soaking leather reins gripped in his other fist. But the horse was still struggling in the wild water, his hooves flailing.

"Pull with me, Elenna," Tom shouted.

Silver ran up and down the bank, barking and whining, as Elenna put

her arms around Tom's waist. Together
they tried to drag Storm closer to the
bank. But it was no good.

"Come on, Storm," Tom urged. His
legs were trembling with exhaustion
as he fell to his knees and gazed at
his stallion.

Storm's eyes were wide and scared
as the water rushed past him. He was
beginning to lose the battle.

"Steady," Tom murmured, almost
as if he were talking to himself. "Stay
calm. Stay calm…"

He repeated the words over and
over again, clicking his tongue,
and gradually Storm's terrified eyes
focused on him again.

Then, one step at a time, the stallion
heaved himself through the water.
At last, with a final, huge effort, he
scrambled on to the riverbank.

Tom threw his arms around his

horse. "Well done, Storm," he gasped, burying his face in the stallion's damp neck. He could feel himself grinning. "You did it, boy."

Elenna fell on Storm's neck and hugged the stallion fiercely. "Oh, Storm," she murmured. "I thought we'd lost you."

Snorting and blowing, Storm quietened. He nuzzled Tom gently, as Elenna rushed to collect long grasses to dry the horse's flanks. They needed to get him dry and warm as quickly as possible.

As Tom unsaddled Storm and rubbed him with the grass, Elenna lit a camp fire. Then Tom draped a blanket around the exhausted stallion. Storm swayed on his feet, as if he were too tired to stand up for much longer. Then he sank gently to the ground beside the fire.

Quickly, Tom stripped off his wet clothes and wrapped himself in another blanket. His clothes would dry overnight beside the flames. Meanwhile, Silver brought Elenna a rabbit he had caught on the riverbank.

"Is the feast to your liking?" Tom joked, offering Elenna a piece of bread and cheese as the rabbit roasted in the embers of the fire.

Elenna tore into the bread. "It'll do," she said between mouthfuls, and smiled.

Later Tom and Elenna ate the

rabbit beside the crackling fire. The rushing sound of the water was comforting now.

"Let's hope we don't have any more water challenges for a while," Elenna sighed.

Tom lay back and stared at the night sky overhead. It was dotted with bright stars, and the moon was almost full. His thoughts drifted to his father, Taladon, who had once undertaken a Beast Quest of his own. He wondered where he was now.

Then he realised that, at this moment, Elenna, Storm and Silver were the closest thing to a family that he had. He never wanted to risk losing any of them again.

CHAPTER THREE

INTO THE DARK JUNGLE

The next morning dawned clear and still. To Tom's relief, Storm seemed rested and calm after his ordeal in the water. Tom and Elenna breakfasted on fresh fish that Elenna caught in the waters of the Winding River. Silver bounded away as they ate, returning with another plump rabbit for himself.

"Time to go," said Tom at last.

Elenna doused the fire and packed her belongings. Tom knew she was thinking about the Beast they were about to face. If he was honest, he was thinking about it as well. What sort of a creature would Claw be?

They soon found a road which led away from the Winding River. As they journeyed on, the valley walls grew steeper and the vegetation more lush. Silver ran on ahead, as clouds chased each other across the stripe of blue sky above their heads.

After a while the road dwindled to a stony track, potholed in places. It was clear that few people came this way. The thought made Tom feel uncomfortable. If the rumours about the Dark Jungle were true, what chance did they have of defeating Claw and finding the golden chainmail?

The stony track began to climb.

Panting, Storm trudged up the steep incline, Silver padding quietly by his side. The sun beat down hard on Tom and Elenna's backs. The air felt close.

The track ended abruptly as they reached the top of a hill. Before them lay a sea of green trees. It stretched as far as the horizon.

"The Dark Jungle," Elenna said in awe. "It's bigger than I'd imagined."

The jungle was vast. Above the trees, the air shimmered with heat. The only way down to the jungle's edge was straight across a marshy stretch of ground. Mosquitoes whined though the air. Storm flicked his ears as the insects darted in to bite where they could.

Tom's heart raced with a mixture of fear and excitement as he clicked his tongue and urged Storm forward. Batting at the insects, they struggled on to the edge of the jungle.

Soon they were facing a dense wall of trees. Strange screeching sounds could be heard high in the canopy. The air was still and expectant.

"I don't like this," Elenna murmured.

Tom could feel Storm tensing beneath him. He shifted the shield on his arm, bringing it close to his chest. Silver was pacing uncomfortably, his tail low and his ears flattened to his head. It was impossible to ignore the feeling of menace that surrounded the Dark Jungle.

Taking out Aduro's map, Tom studied it once more. The golden dot of the chainmail had moved again. Now it looked very close to where they were standing. Tom squinted through the trees.

"We have no choice, Elenna," he said, rolling up the map. "We have to go in. We need to defeat all the Beasts and collect every piece of the golden armour before we can rescue Aduro."

Tom thought again about the kindly wizard. He swallowed.

"We have to rescue him," he said firmly, and urged Storm forward.

The four Questers took their first steps into the Dark Jungle. Tom immediately noticed the stifling heat. It was hard to breathe and he felt the pressure on his lungs. Storm shook his head nervously, while Silver growled softly. Fleshy jungle plants hung all around them. The air was thick and sticky with their strange and powerful scents.

"I have never seen plants like these," Elenna said in wonder. She stretched out her hand to touch a red trumpet-shaped flower.

Immediately the flower snapped

closed and, before Elenna could react, snake-like tendrils wrapped themselves around her arm.

"Tom!" she shrieked.

Tom pulled out his sword and slashed the tendrils away. "Touch nothing," he warned, glancing around. He half-expected to see Malvel himself, laughing from the treetops.

The air grew thicker and darker as they pressed on, and the ground became wetter. Soon Storm was wading cautiously through dark, stinking water, his hooves sliding in the mud, his nostrils flaring at the unfamiliar scents.

"It's OK," Tom soothed, and stroked his horse's mane.

Halfway across the swamp, Tom dismounted. He did not want to be responsible for Storm sinking into the uncertain ground. Elenna did the same and pressed ahead with Silver.

The water was unpleasantly warm and sucked at his legs. Gritting his teeth, Tom took Storm's reins and led the stallion gently onwards. His eyes darted around, checking for signs of the Beast.

Elenna was waiting for them on the far side of the swamp, Silver at her side. She was cutting away the leeches which had attached themselves to her flesh, then she did the same for Tom and Storm.

They moved on, wet and tired.

At last, they emerged into a sun-dappled open space.

A group of chattering monkeys suddenly swung down through the vines. Silver barked furiously and Storm reared in surprise.

Tom and Elenna dived on to the jungle floor in fright.

"Stay down, Elenna!" Tom said, reaching for his sword.

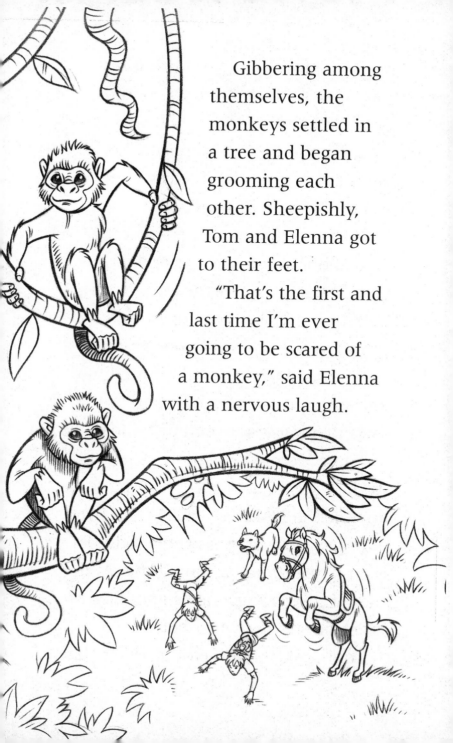

Gibbering among themselves, the monkeys settled in a tree and began grooming each other. Sheepishly, Tom and Elenna got to their feet.

"That's the first and last time I'm ever going to be scared of a monkey," said Elenna with a nervous laugh.

They moved on, Tom using his sword to slash through the damp green undergrowth.

Suddenly Elenna stopped. "Look," she said, pointing at a series of deep gashes in the tree trunks.

"Something has happened here," Tom said slowly, inspecting several huge chunks gouged out of the undergrowth. Torn branches littered the ground. Storm gave a high, anxious whinny.

Elenna picked up something limp and tattered. "A strip of linen," she said, turning it over in her hand.

There were several more strips of cloth scattered across the clearing. Tom and Elenna looked at each other. Even after facing seven Beasts, the sight of such destruction was unsettling. And the torn linen suggested something more sinister than ever before.

Tom took the piece of cloth. "What

could have done this?" he said.

Just then they heard a rustling behind them. Tom and Elenna whirled around, as a claw that was bigger than both of their heads swiped at them from high up in the trees. It was attached to a long, furry tail.

Tom pushed Elenna out of the way, and they tumbled to the ground.

A chill settled on Tom's heart.

It was the Beast. And now the Beast knew they were here.

CHAPTER FOUR

CLAW ON THE ATTACK

Tom peered up into the canopy of trees. It was almost impossible to see anything against the glare of the sun. Leaves rustled and brushed against each other. The Dark Jungle sounded as if it were laughing at its visitors.

A stench of old meat and sweat drifted down through the branches, stronger than the sickly scents of the jungle flowers.

Tom peered up again. But it was no use. The Beast was too high up.

"If only I could see more clearly," he said, frustrated. Then he remembered the golden helmet!

Quickly he pulled it from Storm's saddlebag and put it on, gazing through the slits of the visor up into the treetops again. Now he was able to see the gorgeous greens and vivid colours of the highest point of the jungle.

Then Tom spotted the Beast. He felt his eyes widen in disbelief.

Claw was an enormous monkey. His chest was as wide as Storm was long, and his limbs were thicker than some of the tree trunks around them. He sat hunched among the branches, a hideous creature with a lethal-looking claw at the tip of his long, snake-like tail. Huge, hairy black arms, legs and feet ended in vicious, curved

claws. His face was covered in matted
black hair, but his squashed snout was
hairless. Drool hung in ropes from his
long teeth. And his fierce yellow eyes
were trained directly on Tom.

He knew they had to run. There
was no choice.

"Jump up here, Elenna!" Tom cried, leaping on to Storm and throwing the helmet back into the safety of the saddlebag.

Elenna flung herself into the saddle behind him, scrabbling for a grip, and Tom wheeled the stallion around so hard that Storm reared and nearly fell.

But before the stallion could take them to safety, a torrent of twigs, branches and vines plunged down from the canopy, knocking Tom and Elenna from the saddle. Claw gave a screech of triumph.

Tom tried to struggle to his feet but the weight of the twisted vines was pressing down on him, like an enormous tangled net. Storm neighed in terror and Silver snarled.

"I can't move!" Elenna cried.

The more they twisted, the more tightly the vines drew around them.

The stench of the Beast was everywhere. Tom's arms were pinned down; he couldn't reach his sword.

Claw screeched again. Then, to Tom's horror, the Beast's long, clawed tail swung down and plucked Elenna into the air, ripping the tangled vines away from her with ease.

"Tom!" screamed Elenna.

"No!" Tom cried. He fought to escape, but there was nothing he could do.

Elenna kicked and yelled, as the Beast pulled her up into the trees. Her arms flailed, hitting out uselessly at her captor. "Tom!" she screamed again. "Help me!"

Then there was a sudden awful silence. Where had the Beast taken her?

With a snarl, Silver ripped himself free with his teeth, before tearing at the vines around Tom.

"That's it, boy!" Tom shouted, struggling to free his arms. "Nearly there!"

At last, he could move his arms. Bursting free, he withdrew his sword and thrust it fiercely into the air.

"While there's blood in my veins," he vowed, "I'll save my friend!"

Quickly, he cut away the vines that

still bound Storm's legs. The stallion waited patiently as Tom tugged him free.

Claw had left a trail of destruction in his wake – broken branches and scattered leaves on the jungle floor – so it would be easy to follow him. But Tom needed to approach the Beast with care if he was to save Elenna.

Picking up the scent of his mistress, Silver threw back his head and started to howl.

"No!" Tom cried, running to the wolf. He patted the animal's thick fur and shushed him. Noise was the last thing Tom needed.

But it was too late. Behind him, Tom heard a tell-tale rustling. He looked over his shoulder, hooking a protective arm around Silver.

The Beast's huge shadow spread across the clearing. Claw was back, high in the trees once more. There was no sign of Elenna. Where was she?

Tom tensed as the clawed tail flew down through the branches once again. He dived out of the way, but the claw violently slapped Silver and Storm to one side, and Tom lost sight of them. He hoped desperately that they were all right, and concentrated on the branches, waiting for the tail to reappear.

It lashed towards him suddenly.

Tom ducked, desperate to evade the cruel claw at its tip. The Beast remained in the trees. It was impossible for Tom to see more than his tail.

Claw gibbered and whirled his tail again. This time, Tom reached out and grabbed hold of it. He held on tightly.

"Come down, you coward!" Tom yelled, tugging at the Beast in an effort to bring him crashing to the ground.

The great monkey simply lifted his tail. Yanked off his feet, Tom went flying through the air.

Tom clung on with all his strength, as Claw's tail whipped and thrashed around. The Beast roared and leapt from tree to tree. Tom swung beneath him, jagged twigs and branches tearing at his clothes. The breath was knocked out of him as the Beast slammed him into trees and dragged him through curtains of vines that scratched his face.

This was it. There was no way out.

He wasn't going to escape from the Dark Jungle alive!

CHAPTER FIVE

FALLING

Tom couldn't hold on much longer. His clothes were torn to shreds. His arms and legs were black with bruises. He knew he had to let go.

Timing it as best he could, Tom released his hold on the Beast's tail and plummeted downwards. Stretching out for the nearest tree, his fingers snagged on a branch and he swung there, breathless but safe.

Above him Claw stood up, thumped his vast chest and shrieked at the sky. The treetops shook.

His hands scratched and numb, Tom nearly lost his grip on the branch, but managed to wrap his legs around the tree trunk. For the first time, he could see all of Claw, as the Beast swung from tree to tree above him. The strange movement of the golden dot on Aduro's map suddenly made sense.

The chainmail was draped around Claw's neck.

Tom gasped with wonder at the sight. The piece of armour shimmered magically. The links seemed too fine to be made of metal, and made Tom think of golden silk, knotted into a pattern that sparkled in the light.

Suddenly Claw dropped down through the trees and lunged at Tom again. The Beast's cruel lips were drawn back, revealing his horrible, grinning fangs. Tom grabbed his sword and fought as hard as he could, but it was almost impossible to keep a grip on the tree while he swung his blade. The trees weren't his natural home. Claw was at a huge advantage.

The clawed tail shot towards him once again. This time, it knocked Tom's sword out of his hand. Tom watched in horror as his weapon spiralled down to the ground and out of sight. Now he was defenceless.

He risked a glance at the jungle floor. It seemed a long way down, but his position on the tree trunk was dangerous. He shifted his shield further on to his back, trying to get a better grip on the branch.

"Think, Tom," he told himself fiercely.

Then it came to him.

Onto his shield was fixed the eagle's feather that Arcta the mountain giant had given him. It protected him from great heights.

Pulling his shield from his back, he held it above him.

Then he took a deep breath and jumped.

Vines and branches whistled past, but Tom felt the power of the shield protecting him. His fall was slowing.

Even so, he hit the ground hard, the breath knocked out of him. Within moments, he was buried in the undergrowth. To his relief, his sword lay nearby. He stretched out a hand and grabbed it.

Claw shrieked once more, the sound echoing around the jungle. Then silence fell. It seemed that the Beast had given him up for dead.

Tom lay as still as he could, the comforting weight of the sword in his hand. His first thoughts were for Storm and Silver. He hadn't seen them since the Beast had knocked them aside with his tail. Had they survived? His heart lurched as he glanced around.

Then he heard Storm neigh. The ground beneath him trembled as the stallion cantered towards him with Silver close at his heels.

Storm nudged him and whinnied.

"Hush," Tom whispered, reaching up and stroking Storm's nose. "I'm all right."

He peered through the leaves over his head. There was nothing in the canopy above him. Tom climbed to his feet. He could hardly believe that he had no broken limbs.

He looked at his shield and offered silent thanks to Avantia's great Beasts who had given him their tokens of power, now set deep into the wooden face of the shield: Ferno's dragon-scale protected him from heat, Sepron's tooth from onrushing water, and Nanook's bell from extreme cold. Tagus's horseshoe fragment gave him extra speed and Epos's golden talon healed wounds. And, of course, Arcta's eagle feather, which protected him from great heights, had just saved his life.

Hacking his way free from the undergrowth was almost as difficult as freeing himself from the vines.

The ferns of the Dark Jungle were thick and strong, and curled around him.

Then Tom felt something tickling his leg. He looked down.

A snake was coiled around his knee. Its green-brown skin gleamed in the dim jungle light. Every now and again, a thin black tongue flickered and was gone again. Its yellow eyes were fixed on Tom.

Without taking his eyes off the snake, Tom knocked the creature into the air with the tip of his sword and sliced through its body. The snake's scaly coils twitched and fell to the ground in two pieces. Tom sighed with relief.

Silver pressed his nose to the ground. His ears pricked and he whined. He had picked up Elenna's scent again!

Tom leapt into Storm's saddle. It was time for battle.

We're coming, Elenna! he thought. *Just hold on!*

Silver took off, following the scent. Broken branches dangled from the trees above them as Tom and Storm galloped through the jungle after the wolf. The Beast had cut a path through the canopy that was easy to follow.

Stumbling and slipping, they raced past trunks as thick as ten men. Storm darted between trees and beneath vines, taking sharp turns and following the wolf. Alert for signs of danger, Tom watched the trees and clutched his sword.

It wasn't long before the tangle of trees cleared a little. Silver bounded forward and Storm tossed his head as Tom pressed his heels into the stallion's flanks, encouraging him to gallop faster.

But something was wrong with the path in front of them. The land ahead seemed to be falling away. Storm stiffened as Tom desperately reined him in.

"Silver!" Tom cried. "Look out!"

The wolf twisted his body sharply. But it was too late. Tom watched in horror as Silver went skidding over the edge – and out of sight!

CHAPTER SIX

INTO THE VOLCANO

Tom flung himself off Storm and ran to the edge of the precipice. An enormous hole in the ground lay before him. Tom felt a tremor run through his body. He had seen something like this before, when he had freed Epos the flame bird from Malvel's curse. Only that chasm had been blazing with lava and smoke. This was rich with plant life.

It was the crater of a vast, extinct volcano.

Tom remembered the horrors of his battle to free Epos. He had come close to falling into the boiling lava because he had moved too near the crater's border, where the ground was loose. This time, he sank to his knees and crawled to the edge.

Far below, the heart of the crater was as dark as night. Trees grew tall, reaching up towards the blue sky, desperate for light. It was almost impossible to make out the ground beneath the luxuriant canopy of leaves.

There was no way that Silver could have survived the fall.

But then Tom caught sight of the wolf's silvery pelt. His heart leapt with joy as he saw Silver crouched below him, on a nearly invisible ledge beneath the lip of the crater. Somehow the wolf had stopped himself from falling any further.

Silver stood on his back legs as Tom reached out to him, nosing thankfully at Tom's hand. The ledge was at an awkward angle, tucked underneath the overhang where Tom lay. Reaching down, Tom sank his fingers into Silver's thick pelt and grasped hold of the loose folds of skin around the wolf's neck. He heaved with all his might, and the wolf scrambled out.

"Good boy," Tom murmured, rubbing Silver's head. He felt faint with relief.

The wolf suddenly pulled away from Tom. He ran to the edge of the precipice again, pacing nervously near the edge, sniffing at the air. He growled softly and looked at Tom with his brown eyes.

"What is it?" Tom said, his heart filling with hope.

Silver whined and paced close to the crater, stopping just short of the edge. Stones broke away and bounced down the sheer slope, out of sight.

The golden helmet would help Tom see what Silver had scented. He ran to Storm and lifted the helmet from the saddlebag once more. Then he placed it on his head and gazed back down at the crater.

He could see brightly coloured beetles and sleeping snakes, and every leaf was pinpoint clear. Tom's eyes swept the ground again. Then, through a crack in the canopy, he spotted Elenna in the gloom at the heart of the crater itself.

She was sitting on the ground, her head in her arms. Scattered around her were piles of gleaming white

bones, picked clean. It was Claw's
lair, the place he brought his victims.
She looked unhurt, but she was
trapped at the bottom of the crater.

Tom's head was whirling. He had to defeat Claw and get the chainmail – only by completing the suit of golden armour piece by piece could he rescue Aduro. But first, he needed to save Elenna.

"You can do this!" Tom told himself. "Take it one step at a time."

He glanced around, looking for the Beast. He didn't want Claw to know he had found Elenna. Then he gave a long, low whistle to catch his friend's attention. The Beast was less likely to hear him that way.

Elenna looked up. The thick canopy of leaves was blocking her view of Tom. He whistled again. Getting to her feet, Elenna moved to a piece of clear ground – and grinned with relief when she saw him.

Tom placed a finger on his lips, warning her to stay quiet. He could smell Claw's stench; the Beast wasn't far away. Shadows danced on the ground from the branches high above, playing tricks on Tom's eyes. He whirled about, his eyes darting from shadow to shadow. Where was the giant monkey?

At last, Tom spotted him. High in the canopy above Tom's head, Claw's long, clawed tail swung lazily back and forth. It looked as if the creature was asleep. The chainmail glimmered and clinked around his neck. The sound made Tom think of tiny bells. His heart quickened. The armour seemed to call out to him, shining softly in the sunlight. Tom hesitated, glancing back at the crater.

Elenna first, he thought.

He looked at the vertical walls of the precipice. There was no way down or up. And it was too deep for any of the nearby vines to reach the bottom. Tom was at a loss.

He had no idea how to rescue Elenna.

A hissing sound made him look down. Elenna was gesturing something. At last, Tom realised what she wanted – her bow and arrow!

Tom began a careful sweep of the ground where Claw had dragged Elenna to his lair. Silver kept watch at the mouth of the crater while Storm quietly cropped the grass.

At last, Tom spotted the familiar leather quiver holding Elenna's arrows. Beside it lay her bow. They hadn't fallen into the crater. But they were teetering dangerously close to the edge.

Tom reached for the weapons, but they were just too far from his grasp. He couldn't creep any closer to the edge, or he would tumble over and all would be lost. He watched in dismay as a gust of wind caused the quiver to see-saw gently over the chasm. There wasn't a moment to lose!

Wrapping one hand around a nearby gum tree, Tom leaned as far as he dared towards the weapons. His fingertips brushed the quiver, but he wasn't close enough to grasp it. He uncurled his fingers slightly from the gum tree and dug his toes into the damp ground. A little further… just a little…

Suddenly Tom felt his fingers slip from the gum tree. His toes scrabbled for grip, but it was hopeless. He felt himself toppling and there was nothing he could do.

Tom was falling. The Quest was lost.

"Aduro!" Tom thought. "Aduro, I'm sorry… "

But then, just as he was about to tip over the edge of the crater, something

grabbed his leg and held him fast.
Tom glanced over his shoulder to see
Silver gripping his trouser leg in his
powerful jaws.

Grasping the bow and arrows
firmly in his hand, he rolled back
from the edge of the crater with
a hammering heart.

"Thank you, Silver," he whispered,
throwing his arms around the wolf's

strong neck. "What would I do without you?"

He tied the bow and quiver of arrows together with a vine and threw them down to Elenna. Without a word, she took the arrows in her quiver, fitted them to her bow, and began firing them into the walls of the crater.

Everything became clear as Tom watched where the arrows fell. They had formed a ladder up the crater wall that she could climb to safety.

Tom fell back with a gasp of relief. The ground was cool under his back. He knew how lucky he was to have such a quick-thinking companion on this Quest. Elenna would climb out of the sleeping volcano and then they would face Claw.

Together.

CHAPTER SEVEN

FACING THE BEAST

When he had caught his breath, Tom glanced up into the canopy again. He was still wearing the helmet and could see that Claw remained sleeping, his limbs hanging like thick hairy ropes from the branch overhead, the golden chainmail glinting in the sun. They were still safe – although there was no way of telling for how long.

He wriggled back to the edge of the crater and watched as Elenna stepped up on to the first arrow. It bent slightly beneath her weight, and she struggled to keep her balance.

Tom ran to a nearby tree and cut down a length of vine with his sword. He looped it around a tree trunk and threw the other end to Elenna. It reached halfway down. If she could just get there, he and Silver could pull her up the rest of the way.

Elenna nodded gratefully up at Tom, understanding what he was trying to do. But first she had to get to the vine.

Tom looked on with admiration as his friend grasped the arrow above her head then climbed on to the arrow just below, repeating this movement until she had reached the vine. Each time she took a step up, she reached down to retrieve the arrow she had left behind.

Silver ran back and forth along the mouth of the crater. To Tom's relief, the wolf seemed to know that he should be silent.

Soon Elenna reached the vine and grabbed the end of it. Together, Tom and Silver pulled the vine up the side of the crater. Tom wanted to shout for joy as he felt the grasp of his friend's warm palm.

"We did it!" he whispered fiercely, as he and Elenna swiftly embraced.

They were back together!

But now it was time to face the Beast and retrieve the golden chainmail.

"If I climb into the trees," Tom said in a low voice, "I might take Claw by surprise. It's the only advantage we have."

Elenna nodded, her eyes wide and fearful.

Tom walked to a nearby tree and tested it with his weight.

It was the wrong thing to do.

The tree groaned and started to sway. Then, to Tom's horror, its roots began to rise up from in the soft ground.

"It's dead!" Elenna gasped, backing away as the tree began to topple.

Tom grabbed Storm's bridle, Elenna grasped Silver's pelt, and they all ran clear as the tree thundered to the ground.

The sound boomed around the Dark Jungle.

Then they heard a scream from the canopy.

Claw was awake.

"We just lost our advantage," Elenna panted as she ran.

Tom watched with awe as the Beast leapt from tree to tree, screeching and beating his chest.

"I still have to fight him, Elenna," he said. "I have to get the chainmail."

"I know," Elenna replied unhappily. "But be careful!"

Tom tucked the golden helmet back

into Storm's saddlebag, then gave Elenna his shield. "Use it to protect yourself," he said, setting foot on the sturdiest tree he could see.

Soon he was climbing high into the canopy, his sword swinging awkwardly by his side. Above him, Claw chattered in fury, lashing out with his tail. One hairy black claw was holding on to the chainmail. The Beast had realised what Tom wanted from him.

Tom ducked behind branches as the Beast's razor-sharp tail whistled towards him. Leaves and twigs rained down on the jungle floor. The tree he was climbing shook and shuddered. Grimly, Tom kept scrambling up, then tucked himself into the cleft of a branch and pulled out his sword,

swinging it hard as, once again, the
cruel claw whirled towards him.

Then came a stroke of pure luck:
the base of the branch on which
Claw was standing broke away from
the tree. Screeching, the Beast fell
through the leaves in a flurry of
matted fur and thrashing limbs, his
face contorted with rage.

But as he fell, he lashed out at
Tom's branch.

Tom's heart lurched as the branch splintered beneath him. Instinctively he reached for his shield – and remembered too late that he had given it to Elenna.

Tom fell after the giant monkey, his arms and legs flailing, and landed on a bed of broken branches.

On the ground, barely metres away from him, Claw was lurching wildly from side to side, roaring with anger, and making a clumsy retreat to the nearest tree trunk. But as soon as he leapt on to the tree, his agility and strength seemed to return.

Frustrated and exhausted, Tom prepared to follow. But before he could move Elenna grabbed hold of him.

"Tom!" she said, her eyes alight. "Did you see how Claw couldn't balance on the ground?"

"I thought he had been injured in

the fall," said Tom, as he gazed up at the canopy. "But he seems as strong as ever. Elenna, I don't know how I'm going to do this."

"No," Elenna said. "He wasn't injured. It was his curved claws. They gave him no grip on the forest floor. You can't defeat him *off* the ground – we've both seen how he swings through the trees as if he has wings. But if you can somehow get him *on* the ground, then the fight will be even."

Tom glanced up at the Beast. Elenna was right. His curved claws were perfectly adapted for swinging among the treetops. Walking on the ground was another matter.

But how could they coax Claw down to the jungle floor? It was impossible!

Tom was exhausted now. He groaned. There was no way he could do this on his own.

Dimly he heard Aduro's voice in his head: "Don't give up hope, Tom. Have you forgotten the help you have with you?"

Yes! he thought. *I'm not alone. I have the great Beasts of Avantia on my side.*

Without Sepron the sea serpent's help, Tom knew that they would never have retrieved the golden helmet from Zepha the monster squid. It was time to call on the help of another Beast. And Tom knew exactly who he needed this time. The thought both thrilled and terrified him. For this Beast was one of the mightiest in all of Avantia.

Ferno the fire dragon.

CHAPTER EIGHT

FERNO RETURNS

Tom seized his shield from Elenna and quickly rubbed the dragon-scale set deep into its surface. He felt a rush of exhilaration when he heard Ferno's roar. It filled the air with heat. The sky above the jungle shimmered. Creatures in the darkness of the jungle shrieked in fear and fled.

The mighty dragon of Avantia soared over the jungle canopy, creating a ring of fire in the top branches of the nearby trees, his black leathery wings beating hard, his eyes glowing red in his coal-black face.

Exhilarated at the sight of their old friend, Elenna and Tom clung together and watched as smoke began to fill the already stifling jungle.

The air darkened. Branches crackled. Trees exploded.

Claw was being smoked out!

The Beast screamed his defiance at the dragon. He swung from a branch with one massive arm and beat his chest with the other. But it was a useless display. Ferno swooped again. The blazing fires gleamed on his polished scales. Claw bellowed and fled through the canopy.

Ferno flew above the giant monkey, following his progress through the branches. The dragon's

tail struck the trees and brought
them crashing down in the giant
monkey's path. Screeching parrots
fluttered into the air, their vivid
colours dulled by the smoke.
Everywhere, the tops of the trees
were burning.

"Go, Ferno!" Elenna screamed.

Tom willed the dragon on with all his heart.

Claw couldn't fight much longer. The Beast was struggling for breath, his chest heaving, as he held his great curved claws over his head, batting uselessly at the smoke. It was everywhere, curling and billowing through the sky. The only place that remained smoke-free was the jungle floor. In desperation, Claw dropped to the ground, snarling.

As soon as the Beast landed, Tom struck, his sword flashing, his shield protecting his head. Claw stumbled, trying to get away, but his clawed feet weren't quick enough. Tom gave chase, leaping through the undergrowth. The Beast hobbled pitifully, stumbling and groaning.

Elenna unleashed a volley of arrows. Claw howled in pain.

"Go, Silver!" she shouted.

The wolf nipped at the Beast's legs in a whirl of silver fur, and Storm joined the fight, his hooves sharp and deadly.

With the help of his friends, Tom closed the gap between himself and the Beast.

Claw was cornered.

The giant monkey curled back his horrible lips. The sight of his putrid yellow fangs was terrifying. Tom thrust hard with his sword, aiming for the clasp on the golden chainmail, which still hung around the Beast's neck. He had to get it – whatever it took.

But Claw was not helpless after all. The great clawed tail slashed through the air and flicked him away. Tom tried again. And again the Beast's tail knocked him away. No matter how

Tom approached, he could not reach the chainmail with his sword.

Desperate to distract the giant monkey, Tom whistled sharply for Storm. As the stallion crashed through the foliage, Claw reared back and Tom seized his chance. He raced up close, moving his shield to his back, and leapt onto a nearby branch to raise himself to the level of the Beast's neck. Then, in the blink of an eye, he slid the tip of his sword into the chainmail's clasp and pulled. It half-opened.

Then the giant monkey's eyes flicked back to Tom and he lunged forward, wrapping his tail around Tom's waist. Tom stared with panic into the Beast's foul face as he felt himself being lifted into the air, his feet dangling above the ground. The tail's grip grew tighter as Tom struggled. He could feel his insides

being crushed. His sword arm was
pinned to his side, the weapon
useless. The Beast prepared to leap
once again into the few remaining
trees that weren't yet burning.

"No!" Tom bellowed helplessly.

Then he heard Storm whinnying a high-pitched challenge and turned to see Elenna galloping towards him on the black stallion, a splintered tree branch in her hand. She aimed the sharp tip of the branch at Claw, and hurled it like a javelin. It crashed into the half-open clasp on the chainmail and loosened it still further.

Claw's grip slackened and Tom crashed back onto the jungle floor, gulping deep breaths. There was no time to check for injuries. Every second counted.

Claw had dropped from the trees again. Screaming at Tom, the hideous Beast's tail whipped through the air.

"Ferno!" Tom shouted in desperation, holding his shield above his head.

The huge, scaly head of the fire dragon darted down through

the trees. Tom caught a glimpse of a blood-red eye. A jet of fire plumed from Ferno's mouth, bounced off the shield and hurtled towards Claw.

Like lightning, the giant monkey pulled back its tail and leapt back, gibbering in fear, as Ferno's flames consumed the ground in front of him. All around, the trees were burning fiercely. The shield protected Tom from heat, but he and his friends would soon be choked by the smoke.

"Again, Ferno!" Tom called, as his eyes stung and watered in the thick grey air.

Ferno roared, and there was another jet of bright flame. Elenna screamed. Tom almost fell backwards as he felt the force of the fire hurtle into the shield and change direction – straight towards the Beast.

CHAPTER NINE

VICTORY

Claw screeched, lurching away from the flames. There was nowhere left for him to go. The trees all around were burning, opening great charred gaps to the sky. The Beast fell to his knees. Tom threw himself at Claw's exposed neck and tore open the loosened clasp. At last, the golden chainmail slithered to the ground.

Ferno's roar shook the jungle. One last column of fire, as wide as a tree trunk, blasted into the ground, hiding Claw behind a thick black cloud of smoke.

Stiffly, Tom reached for his sword again, ready to protect everything that he held dear.

The smoke began to clear. But where the great shaggy body of Claw should have been, something extraordinary met Tom's eyes.

A group of small, excitable monkeys were clustered together on the ground. They chattered, jumped into the lower branches of the unburnt trees, and happily groomed each other.

Where had the Beast gone?

Elenna looked as puzzled as Tom felt. He gazed again at the empty space where Claw had cowered just a few seconds earlier. Then he stared back at the trees where the monkeys were sitting. He'd never seen anything quite like it before.

Then he realised it was all over. He collapsed to his knees, his lungs suddenly raw. Dimly he heard Elenna's voice.

"Tom!" she called. "Tom, you've done it!"

Ferno gave a piercing cry. Tom looked up. Above the burnt wreckage of the Dark Jungle, the vast wings of the dragon were beating.

"Thank you, Ferno," he whispered.

The dragon cried again, a sweet but fierce sound that Tom knew he would never forget. As Tom watched, he swooped away. Soon Ferno was no more than a black speck in the distance.

The next thing he saw was Elenna's face, grimy and bright with triumph.

"The chainmail, Tom!" she said.
"It's yours!"

Climbing slowly to his feet, Tom
stumbled over to the golden chainmail,
the second piece of the precious
armour. It was warm to the touch. He
lifted it up, almost staggering at its
weight. For a moment, he panicked. It
was too heavy. He would never be able
to lift it over his shoulders.

But as he did, the links slithered into place. Immediately, Tom became aware of a magic pulse in his chest, and the chainmail became as light as a feather. Energy surged into his tired muscles. He felt as brave as a lion.

He looked at Elenna, who was standing in the clearing with Storm and Silver at her side. "Extra strength of heart," he murmured, stroking the chainmail. "The helmet gives me sharper sight, and the chainmail makes me feel as if I could face any battle. I could fight ten new Beasts right now, Elenna. Twenty!"

Elenna grinned. "Well done, Tom."

"I would never have called Ferno if you hadn't suggested that we had to fight Claw on the ground," Tom admitted.

"Hey," said Elenna, looking pleased. "I always knew I was the brains in this team."

Storm whinnied softly and pushed at Tom's hand. Tom stroked the stallion's dusty black coat, as Silver lay panting at Elenna's feet.

Then he took off the chainmail and laid it gently across Storm's back. Tiredness seeped back into his muscles. "Now I could sleep for a week," he said. "But we still have four more pieces of armour to find, and four more Beasts to defeat. And Aduro..."

His voice trailed away. Soberly, Elenna met his gaze. Was King Hugo's wizard still alive? Was he holding out against Malvel's evil magic?

"We must leave this place," Tom said. "We have to finish the Quest as quickly as we can so that we can rescue Aduro."

They began walking back the way they had come. Everything looked different, blackened and twisted by the force of Ferno's fire.

Soon they reached the thick green trees in the heart of the Dark Jungle. Ferno's flames had not touched this place. They moved slowly through the maze of plants and vines. Monkeys, small and unthreatening, chattered and swung through the branches above them.

"Watch out for snakes," Tom warned Elenna, remembering the snake he had killed. "They are everywhere."

Suddenly there was a strange thickening in the air.

"You'll have to watch out for more than that," came a mocking voice.

Tom gasped. He reached for his sword as a shimmering image of Malvel appeared against the canopy of leaves above them.

"We have two pieces of the golden

armour, Malvel!" Tom shouted
defiantly. "We defeated Claw! It
won't be long before we find you
and rescue Aduro – and then there
will be nothing you can do."

"You will not be so sure of yourself
when you meet the next evil Beast –
Soltra," said Malvel.

"Where is Aduro?" Tom challenged.

Malvel laughed, a sneering sound
that echoed around the jungle. His

image faded. In its place, Tom saw the great jungle crater they had left behind. Lying among the white animal bones was a scrap of red cloth.

"Aduro's cloak is red," said Elenna, her voice filled with anger. "What have you done with him, Malvel? If you have harmed him…"

The sound of Malvel's laughter filled the air once more as the image of the crater receded, and Tom felt something brush past him. He whirled around, but could see nothing.

"Good luck," the voice of Malvel whispered in his ear. It felt like the cold touch of a bat's wing. "You and your team of nobodies. When you see what still lies in store on this Quest, you'll need it…"

Tom gripped his sword, feeling the comforting weight of his shield on his back. He remembered the golden helmet in Storm's saddlebag and glanced at the golden chainmail that lay across the stallion's broad back. They were not alone. The Beasts of Avantia were on their side, and with every evil Beast he defeated he gained one more piece of the precious armour. His powers were growing.

"We'll be ready!" he vowed, thrusting his sword into the air. "Whatever it takes, Malvel, while there's blood in my veins, we will defeat you!"

Join Tom on the next stage
of the Beast Quest

Meet

SOLTRA
THE STONE
CHARMER

Can Tom and Elenna collect the
golden armour and free Avantia?

PROLOGUE

It had been a long day for the farmer. He plodded along the earth furrows behind his two oxen. Sweat dripped down his neck as he guided the heavy plough through the soil.

The sun was setting over the marsh that lay to the west of the farm. The farmer looked up, then frowned, lifting an arm to mop his brow. Dense fog was beginning to creep from the marsh across the field. It was unusual for it to be so thick at this time of year.

Shivering a little, he unharnessed the oxen and began to lead them towards the stable. The animals were usually eager for their meal at day's end, but now the farmer could hardly get them to move. He snapped the leather harness, then frowned. The harness had become icy cold in his fingers. He turned. The two oxen had come to a dead halt.

"What's wrong, lads?" he asked, walking back to them. Tendrils of fog encircled them all, cutting them off from the farmhouse. He patted the neck of one ox, then let out a shocked gasp. Instead of warm flesh, his hand had struck a hard, cold surface.

The two animals had turned to stone!

As he looked into the oxen's great brown eyes – which were still moving, wide and rolling with fear – he saw a shadowy, milky outline reflected in them. Something or someone was standing right behind him.

He turned, crying out in fear as he stared at the female figure that had stepped from the heart of the fog. The setting sun glowed behind her.

The woman was two heads taller than him, her body swathed in a shining, rippling garment – like a cloak made of black water. He gazed up into the woman's face – but found that she had no face, just a featureless surface, marble smooth and milky white.

Then the final terror came.

The whole of the face folded up on itself like a huge eyelid – and from beneath that eyelid stared a single great eye, as green and clear as an emerald.

He stared into the unblinking eye and suddenly his fear slipped away.

"Beautiful," he murmured.

"It's...so...beautiful..."

He took a step towards the woman.

She lifted an arm and held out a white hand to him. He grasped it, close enough now to see his own reflection in the great green eye. Crystals of ice filled his veins, deadening his limbs, freezing his heart.

Moments later, like his oxen, only his eyes could move. His body was encased in stone.

The woman turned, her cloak undulating as she drifted back into the fog.

A few moments later, the farmer saw a movement out of the corner of his eye. A small boy was crouching in terror behind the low dry-stone wall that marked the boundary of the field. He tried to call to the boy, to ask him to fetch help, but the only sound that escaped him was a groan.

Terrified, the boy ran towards the village.

The fog curled around the farmer's shoulders like a shroud.

How long, he wondered, would it be before death took him?

CHAPTER ONE

HOMEWARD BOUND

"At last!" gasped Tom as he pushed past
a branch and found himself gazing out over
open countryside.

"Thank goodness!" said Elenna from behind
him. "I was beginning to think the Dark Jungle
went on for ever."

They stepped out into the cool of the late
afternoon, exhausted and glad to be free of the
dark, sultry heat.

Ahead of them, the land sloped downwards
in grassy terraces to a wide, winding river that
rushed through deep stony banks.

Tom took one final glance back into the
sinister jungle, thinking of his battle with Claw,
the giant monkey, and remembering how he
had just managed to snatch the golden
chainmail from the evil Beast.

Silver the wolf and Storm, Tom's noble
stallion, emerged from the jungle, too. Silver
bounded and barked joyfully, and Storm

neighed and pranced.

"They're glad to be out in the open," Elenna said. "Can we camp for the night down by the river? I could catch us some fish for our supper."

Tom looked thoughtfully at her and sighed.

"What's wrong?" she asked.

"I was thinking about Aduro," he replied. "I'm worried about what Malvel might have done to him."

The Dark Wizard had kidnapped their friend and protector, Wizard Aduro, and had appeared to them in a vision after Tom's defeat of Claw, showing them torn strips of Aduro's red cloak. Was the good wizard even still alive?

Whatever fate had befallen Aduro, Tom knew that he had to fulfil his Quest and unite the six parts of the golden armour that Malvel had stolen and scattered across the kingdom. Aduro had told them it was the only way they could rescue him. Only then would the land of Avantia be safe from the six evil Beasts Malvel had set loose.

The friends and their two animal companions made their way to the river. A valley brought them down to a shingled beach.

Tom watched as Elenna waded into the

water with an arrow on her bow. After a long wait, she fired an arrow and a moment later was splashing her way up to the shore with a large salmon. She left it on a rock and went back to catch some more.

Silver sniffed the fish but shook his big shaggy head and trotted off. Tom guessed that he was on the prowl for something he'd find a bit tastier. Storm was grazing contentedly on some tall grass.

Tom felt tired and homesick as he looked at the racing river, thinking how different it was from the wide, still lake beside his home village of Errinel. He had not seen it for a long time now.

He shook himself and started to gather wood. Then he lit a fire. He made two tripods of sturdy twigs and skewered the salmon on another twig to hang it above the flames. Soon Elenna came back with two more fish.

The twilight deepened as the fish cooked, and, as they ate, Tom told Elenna about his home. "The lake is as clear as crystal," he said. "On hot summer evenings everyone goes to the lake's shore to eat, play music and watch the sunset."

"It sounds lovely," Elenna said through

a mouthful of salmon.

"People say that the water has healing properties," Tom continued, gazing at the darkening sky. "The water has to be collected as the sun sets." He laughed. "It's just a legend," he said. "I don't suppose it's true."

"It's a nice story, all the same," Elenna said. "And after all that we've seen, who knows what's true and what isn't? Most people think the Beasts are a myth, but we know they're not."

After they had finished their meal, Tom and Elenna went to check on their companions. Silver was lying with his head between his paws, snoring softly. Storm stood close by, dozing peacefully.

The two friends found a place to spread their bedrolls for the night. The pieces of armour that Tom had already recovered were by his side. The golden helmet, forged into the shape of an eagle's head, gleamed softly in the growing starlight. He reached out and touched the chainmail vest, wondering about the Master of the Beasts who had worn it before him. Then he thought of his father, Taladon the Swift, who had undertaken a Beast Quest of his own many years ago, but had disappeared. "I wish I had known him," he thought drowsily. He hoped that one day they might be reunited.

The next day dawned bright and warm, the sun rising in a clear blue sky. Tom unrolled the magical map of Avantia that Aduro had given him when his adventures first began.

As he studied it, the map came to life. Meadow grass moved in the wind and the tiny mountains were cold to the touch. The forests and rivers, villages and castles were all miniature versions of the real landscape of Avantia.

A glowing red path usually appeared on the map, showing Tom where to journey next, but for the moment there was no sign of it.

"There!" exclaimed Elenna after they had been staring at the map for a little while.

A tiny heart of golden light was glowing on the map. As Tom and Elenna peered, it pulsed and grew larger until they could make out the shape of a golden breastplate.

"It's the next piece of armour!" Elenna said.

Tom let out a cry of delight. "Yes!" he gasped. "And look where it is!" He pointed to a wide clear lake set in rich farmlands. Beside the lake nestled a small village. "It's Errinel, my home! You'll be able to meet Uncle Henry and Aunt Maria, who brought me up." Tom felt his eyes fill with tears. "I haven't seen them since I started the Quests," he said.

A large muzzle snuffled close to his ear. It was Silver, his eyes bright with understanding. Tom turned with a grin. Storm was close by, pawing at the shingle with a hoof.

"You can't hide your feelings from us!" Elenna said with a laugh. "We know how much you want to go home!

"Yes!" Tom laughed. "And no stopping till we get to Errinel!"

But his laughter soon faded as he thought of his Quest and of the dangers that lay ahead. He had to get to Errinel quickly – but what kind of Beast would be waiting there for them?

And what harm had it already done to his home and his family?

Follow this Quest to the end in SOLTRA THE STONE CHARMER.

Win an exclusive
Beast Quest T-shirt and goody bag!

In every Beast Quest book the Beast Quest logo
is hidden in one of the pictures. Find the logos in
book 7 to book 12 and make a note of which pages
they appear on. Send the six page numbers in to us.
Each month we will draw one winner to receive
a Beast Quest T-shirt and goody bag.

Send your entry on a postcard listing the titles
of books 7–12, the winning page numbers in each
book and your name, age and address to:

BEAST QUEST: THE GOLDEN ARMOUR COMPETITION
Orchard Books
338 Euston Road
London NW1 3BH

Australian readers should write to:

Orchard Books Australia
Level 17/207 Kent Street
Sydney, NSW 2000

Only one entry per child.
Final draw: 30 May 2009

You can also enter this competition
via the Beast Quest website: www.beastquest.co.uk

by Adam Blade

Series 1

Series 2: The Golden Armour

All priced at £4.99
Vedra & Krimon: Twin Beasts of Avantia is priced at £5.99

The Beast Quest books are available from all good
bookshops, or can be ordered direct from the publisher:
Orchard Books, PO BOX 29, Douglas IM99 1BQ.
Credit card orders please telephone 01624 836000
or fax 01624 837033 or visit our website: www.orchardbooks.co.uk
or e-mail: bookshop@enterprise.net for details.

To order please quote title, author
and ISBN and your full name and address.
Cheques and postal orders should be made payable to 'Bookpost plc.'
Postage and packing is FREE within the UK
(overseas customers should add £2.00 per book).

Prices and availability are subject to change.